Born and brought up at Eton where her father was a housemaster, Mary Sheepshanks began writing as a child and had her first poem published in the *Sunday Times* at the age of seventeen. She married the headmaster of Sunningdale School while still a very young woman and they ran the school together until 1967 when she and her husband moved up to take over the family estate in Yorkshire. Mary Sheepshanks has three children and a host of grandchildren – one of whom refers to her as his 'wild writing Granny'.

Picking up the Pieces is Mary Sheepshanks' third novel. Her first two, *A Price for Everything* and *Facing the Music*, are also available in Arrow.